For the Kahng and Wiesner families

Special thanks to Carol, Trish, John, Rick, Kevin & Victor for all their help.

Copyright © 2020 by David Wiesner

All rights reserved. For information about permission to reproduce selections from this book, write to trade.permissions@hmhco.com
or to Permissions, Houghton Mifflin Harcourt Publishing Company, 3 Park Avenue, 19th Floor, New York, New York 10016.

Clarion Books is an imprint of Houghton Mifflin Harcourt Publishing Company.
hmhbooks.com

The illustrations in this book were created in watercolor. The text was set in Gill Sans Semibold.
Book design by Carol Goldenberg • Lettering by John Green

Library of Congress Cataloging-in-Publication Data is available.
ISBN 978-0-544-98731-9 hardcover   ISBN 978-0-358-42332-4 signed edition

Manufactured in China
SCP 10 9 8 7 6 5 4 3 2 1
4500797907

ROBOBABY

DAVID WIESNER

Clarion Books / Houghton Mifflin Harcourt / Boston • New York

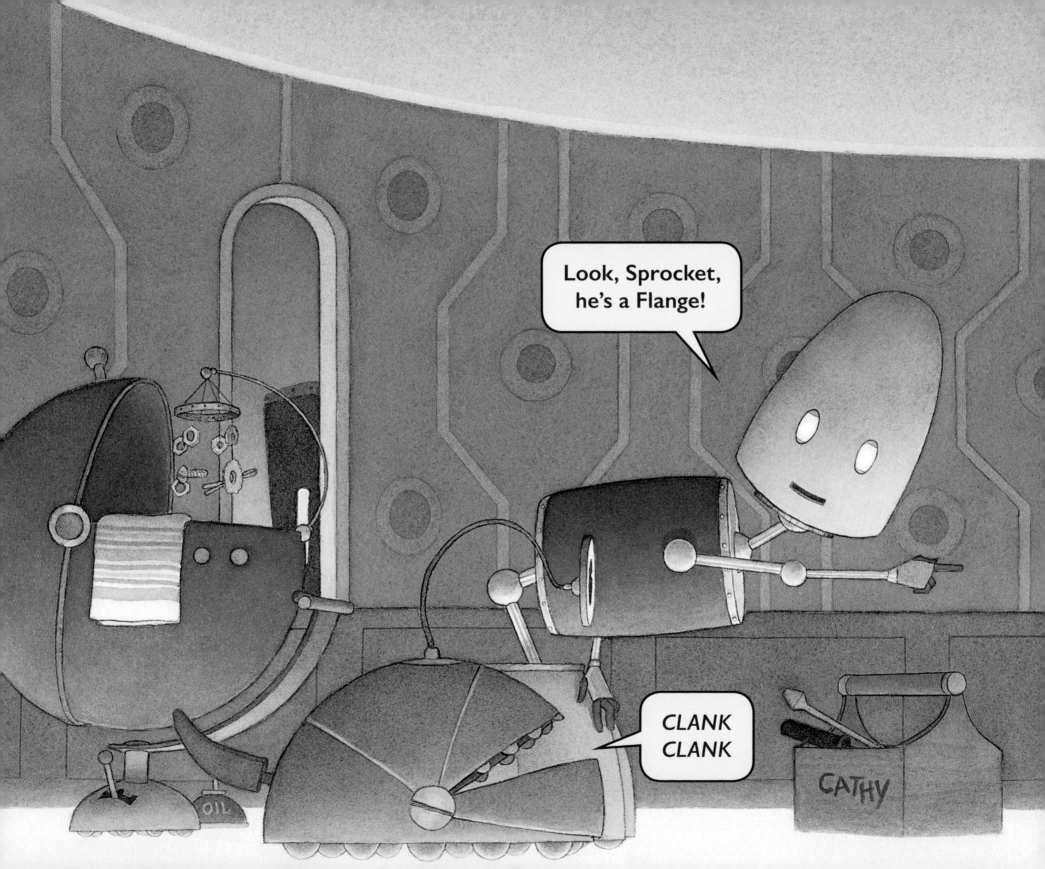

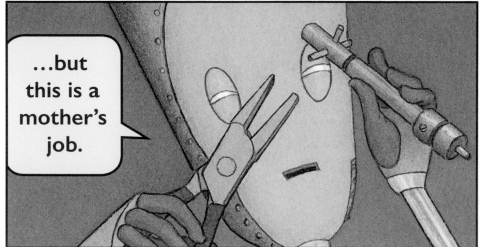

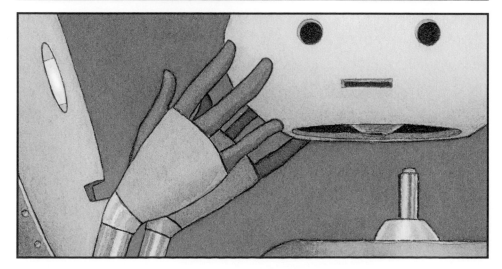

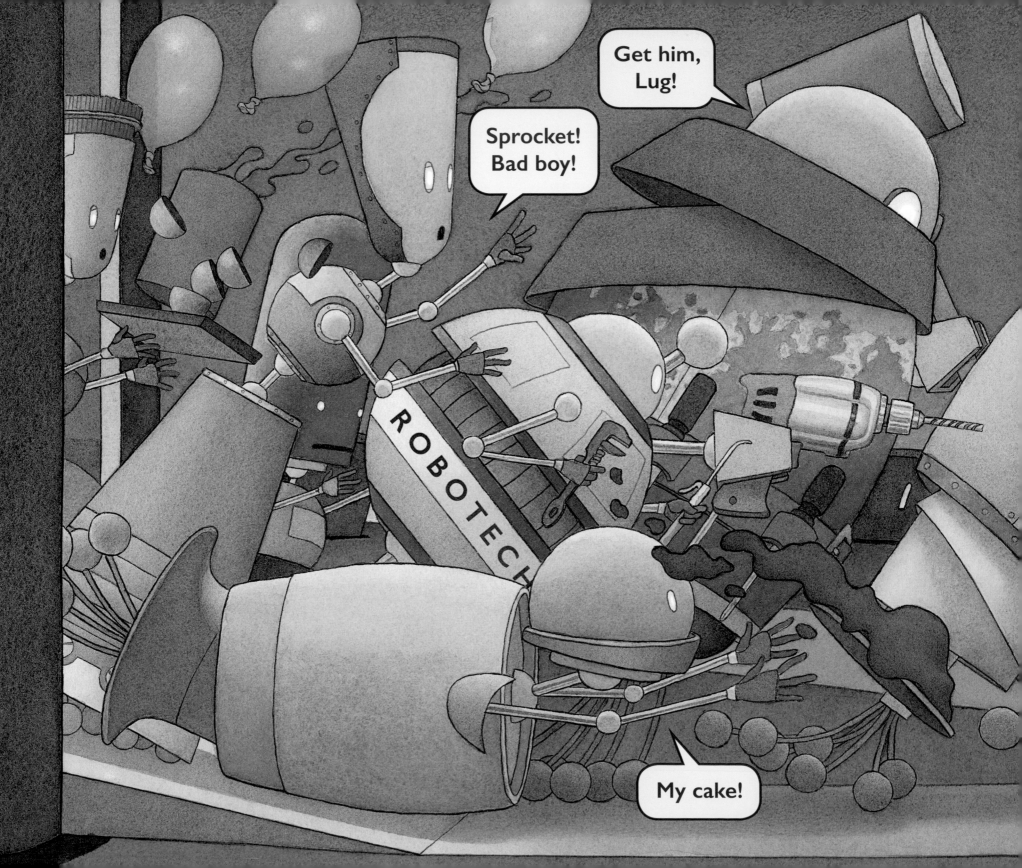